Cyril

the
Short Sighted Caterpillar

The Big Number Two

Written and Illustrated by
Jeremy Faithfull

Image Enhancement by
Earlene Gayle Escalona

To order additional copies of this book, contact:
Xlibris
0800-056-3182
www.xlibrispublishing.co.uk
Orders@ Xlibrispublishing.co.uk

Dedication

for Amanda.
'In Loving memory'
If tears could build a stairway, and memories build a lane, I'd walk right up to heaven, to bring you home again.
"DAD"

Love you always.

Special Acknowledgement
Anya Jorja & Freya Elise,

'They know what they did'.

"Cyril...Ooh is ziss Doofy ze giant walking female keeps calling out to?" Amelie asked Cyril as he slowly crawled around the perimeter of the glass tank, into which Miss Ruby Henderson had so carefully put them.

Like a concertina his back end arched, then slowly it moved towards his midriff, this in turn met his middle...Closely followed by his front end lurching forward searching for the next piece of safe foliage, onto which he could place his front feet of plenty.

"I recognise this place!" Cyril shouted back to Amelie, surprised by his sudden remembrance of the surroundings, "follow me I know my way around here...I think," he added confidently whilst scratching his head, feeling a little bemused. Amelie gingerly made her way towards Cyril, who by now was already busy making himself at home.

"I think an entre of willow leaves with just a splattering of the oak," the greedy little caterpillar thought to himself as he set about eating another pile of leaves. Amelie had a real sense of fear and trepidation as she moved her body against the side of the glass tank.

Phaarp!

She accidentally rubbed her derrière against the glass, making a noise like a rubber balloon being pulled across a window.

Phaarp!...Phaarp!....Phaarp!

Moving ever cautiously, she eventually made it to where Cyril was busy eating more Willow leaves.

"You know you should keep away from the wall that you cannot see!" Cyril went on to explain, "If you touch it, it makes that spine tingling sound".

"What ziss one?" Amelie replied as she deliberately rubbed her bottom against the glass again.

Phaarp!

"Yeess!" Cyril said as he shook with the shiver that was sent travelling down his spine. "You did that on purpose!...How rude!" He called accidentally losing some of the food in his mouth.

"Ooh is Doofy ze giant walking female Keeps calling out to?" Amelie asked Cyril again. "I think it might be me, I think I can remember being called that before," he replied. "Before what? Amelie enquired.

"My daring escape!........Did you not read the book?" Cyril answered in a smug voice. "Book...What is ziss book to which you refer mon ami?" Amelie asked.

"It's a long story," Cyril replied.

"Well we do 'ave plenty of time," Amelie answered as her curiosity began to peak.

"No.., I mean it's a long story, you might even get a mention if you play your cards right!" Cyril said.

"Uh... I do not understand," Amelie answered in a confused tone of voice.

"You will one day....When I'm famous!" Cyril replied in his smuggest of very smug voices. "You have got to taste these oak leaves," Cyril told Amelie, "if you take a bite of this one...Then take a bite of that one and mix it with a mouthful of that one, add a little bit of this one...And then...If you chew it together with Just a smidgeon of that one...It's like the flavours are doing a samba on your tongue!" Cyril rambled, chewing and talking at the same time.

"No!" Shouted Amelie,

"All you do is sink about eating!" She shouted again. "Don't you then?! Cyril snapped back.

"No!" She replied in an angry voice, "We 'ave got to try to get out of 'ere".

"Why would you want to get out of here?..It's paradise, we have a veritable cornucopia of eats and if I remember....Yes!.. There may well be some fruit over there...Well...What do you say?" Cyril asked Amelie all excited 'n' that.

"I say, all you do is sink about food!" Amelie called-out to Cyril.

"But I'm a Caterpillar... it's my job!" Cyril stated, assured in the fact that Amelie would surely have to agree.

"All we have to think about is our bellies...What else is there?" Cyril asked Amelie again. Amelie had no choice but to concur with everything Cyril had said, plus the willow and oak leaves mixed with the fruit did make a mouthful of food to die for.

"Anyway..You're not the boss of me!" Cyril said in a deep voice.

"Do you not sink I know zat mon ami" Amelie replied in a stern voice, "But I could be if I wanted to!" She added abruptly. "Whatever!" Cyril replied.

He turned around and carried on with the job in hand...Late lunch.

"Do not...For one moment sink zat ziss is ze end of it!" Amelie called to Cyril.

"I will not my love..My sweet heart..My darling baby girl," Cyril replied in his most subservient voice.

Amelie and Cyril both began the mammoth task of eating the mountain of food in front of them, the one that Miss Ruby Henderson had so kindly gathered for their consumption. "Cyril Mon amore, you still 'ave not told me 'ow you managed to get out of 'ere," Amelie asked Cyril with a soft tone in her voice.

"Well...There was a big round ball of fluff...It was black and white...I think... And it had two arms with sharp things on the end...Diablo!..It's a Diablo!" Cyril suddenly remembered,

"I think that is what the giant female walker called it anyway". Cyril went onto explain...

"I seem to recall he was a bit of a menace, If my memory serves me well...Walking around like he owns the whole house, It doesn't bother me how sharp the sharp things on the end are,

I could handle him...

If I had to...Easy!...If I had to," he said in a macho, deep voice.

Cyril then took a deep breath..Sucking his belly in he started to explain, "Well I'm starting to get slightly off-track," he added.

"One morning when the big bright thing was high up the giant walking lady dropped off my breakfast...My second breakfast, my brunch, my lunch, my high tea, my tea time snacks and my dinner.

I remember it well, only Just because she had forgotten my second dinner and my supper.. Oh!... And my night-time snacks, but as for the lack of puddings don't even get me started...

I mean...I wouldn't have even minded just a few slices of apple...

Or a juicy bit of melon, I love a slice of melon, sticky, juicy and sweet....mmm," Cyril murmured lovingly.

"Cyril!...'Ow did you get out of 'ere!?" Amelie asked in a firm but comforting voice.

"Try and concentrate," she added, trying to get Cyril to focus on the story.

"Sorry," Cyril replied.

"Where was I...Oh yes the melon, sticky, juicy, sweet and tasty".

Cyril's mind started to wander again..lost in juicy, sweet, sticky melon loveliness.

"Cyril!" Amelie exclaimed, her patience was by now wearing just a little bit thin.

"I was just getting to it!" Cyril quaffed.

"I was just painting a picture with words so you could imagine it like you were there, If you knew how juicy and sticky and sweet that melon was...You would not be so rude and interrupt!" The little green caterpillar added.

"Sorry!".. Amelie replied in a patronizing tone of voice, "I should 'ave been less selfish please continue".

"Fine then!"....Cyril snapped.

"Fine zen!"....Go on zen!"...Amelie answered back.

"Fine then!"...I will then!"...But one more comment and I will stop, I do have better things to do don't you know!...Those Oak leaves and apple slices don't eat themselves you know,

Or those Yew leaves and chopped bananas either, nor the plums and melon slices....Or". "Cyril!" Amelie barked, stopping Cyril in the middle of his sentence.

"No..No.. I'm sorry, Caterpillars don't bark, they can't even talk.... Can they?" The author asks in a curious tone.

"It's a children's book based on creatures from the natural world, It's about a caterpillar that wears glasses...It's not real...Is it?" The author adds quizzically.

"Um hello!...We are still here...And we are not deaf you know!" Amelie and Cyril both said together, addressing the author.

"Sorry... let's get back to the story shall we?" The author writes apologetically.

"Huh-hum," Amelie cleared her throat..

"Cyril!" She calls out in a feminine voice with a French accent. "Ow was zat?" She asks the author.

"It's fine, can we focus...Please!" The author writes, now starting to get a little impatient.

"Cyril!" Amelie called out.

"Where was I...Oh yes the melon slices...Melon...mmmmm," Cyril said. "Cyril! ze story!" Amelie exclaimed.

"You try saying melon without saying mmmm," Cyril argued. "I cannot work like ziss!" Amelie said in a cross voice.

The vein down the centre of her forehead was now starting to throb.

"If you continue in ziss vain I shall walk...I mean it!" She said in a shaky voice close to tears.

"She just said vain...And the vein on her fore head is standing out...That's funny". The author writes, laughing.

"No it is not!" Cyril shouts to the author, "You are talking about the caterpillar I love... If she goes...I go!

No Cyril!...No book!...No book!..No Royalties!...How do you like those onions?" Cyril asks the author.

"It's fine! I will just write a different book...

One that's about a Caterpillar with 20-20 vision perhaps!" The author writes with an assertive tone.

"I could also write-in funny and embarrassing scenarios to put you in!" The Author adds.

"Shall we say"...

A glorious, golden sandy beach, it's a beautiful sunny day..There's a clear blue sky and some children are paddling in the sea.

Some children are sitting building sand castles, others are eating ice creams.

"And Cyril?....Oh yes Cyril".

Cyril is sitting on the beach in a mess of melting ice cream and he is wearing a woman's floppy sun hat.

It's Timmy's eight birthday, many of his friends are sitting around the dinning table. The room is decorated sumptuously with balloons adorning every surface. Some children are eating sandwiches, others are scoffing large slices of cake or quaffing copious amounts of juice.

"And Cyril?...Oh yes Cyril".

Cyril is in the middle of the table contained within a red coloured, Strawberry flavoured Jelly.

"Or I could write,"

It was a clear, warm Saturday evening.

The people in the crowd are sitting under the big top, everyone is excited waiting for the show to start.

The performers enter the big top for the parade, the Ring Master leads a procession of circus performers, there are acrobats, Trapeze Artists, lion Tamers, Elephant Trainers with little monkeys, Gymnasts and Clowns are all joining the throng.

It really is big fun.

"And Cyril?...Oh yes Cyril".

Cyril is at the back of the procession, adorning the bonnet of the clown's car. He looks like he's having fun.....Not!.

Its a cool, clear November night, let's say around seven thirty-ish.
Timmy and his family are enjoying a fun filled evening barbecue with lots of their friends, Some of Timmy's friends are holding sparklers, others are digging into juicy quarter-pound burgers in buns, other more ethical guests are enjoying veggie burgers.
The grown-ups are having baked spuds, "mmmmmm...Spuds!"
"And Cyril?...Oh yes Cyril".
"Cyril is actually....Um.... Where is Cyril?...I can't see where Cyril is...Bear with me for Just one moment...Cyril is just...Oh there he is, If you look down to the bottom of the garden near to where Timmy's dad, Bob is.
Bob is about to light a rocket, If you look carefully...Have you guessed who it is yet?"

It's a beautiful, warm summers day and the suns rays are dancing gently on the waves as they break gently on the sandy beach.

Some small schools of fish flit in and out of the craggy rocks, others play games of hide and seek. Sea Horses dance gracefully along the sea bed.

A flat fish is hiding under the sand waiting for lunch to just swim by.

"And Cyril?...Oh yes Cyril".

Cyril is a Puffer Fish trying hard not to be a bigger fish's lunch!

"Should I continue?"... Are you getting the picture?" The author writes trying not to laugh to much.

"Okay!..Okay!..We get the Idea," Cyril calls out to the author.

"Two Compliant Caterpillars sitting in a tank...One's called Cyril and one's called Amelie, Blah Blah Blah".... The caterpillars both say to the author bluntly.

"Minus the sarcastic tones thank you," The author adds.

"Melons, melons, melons...Oh yes!...Sliced melon," Cyril muttered, lost in his thoughts of melon Juiciness.

"Finally...Thank you," The author sighs.

"I was sitting enjoying my second breakfast, I recall there was a rather large thud, I then looked up from my second breakfast and to my surprise I saw the Diablo, he was hanging from the side of the wall, you know, the one that you cannot see,

I remember thinking...That's a strange thing to happen during second breakfast... That's a strange thing to happen during first breakfast!...Or even dinner really," Cyril continued with his verbal rambling, trying hard to explain his utter confusion with what was occurring.

"Cyril!" Amelie called out, "focus on ze story!"

"Okay okay....I noticed that the flat thing you cannot see had a gap in it and that is how I

escaped...Simple," Cyril said raising his hands and shrugging his shoulders.

"Zat is it!" Amelie replied in an angry voice, "I sought zat it was going to be epic!... Ze story of one Caterpillar's struggle against ze world!" She added feeling a little deflated by Cyril's explanation.

"It was......Mainly," Cyril replied sensing Amelie's dissatisfaction.

Miss Ruby Henderson walked through to her kitchen only to be met by Diablo, her little black and white kitten winding his body between her legs.

"Meeoow...Watch out!..You nearly stepped on me!" Diablo meowed with disdain.

Miss Ruby Henderson was sent stumbling across the kitchen floor.

"Watch out Diablo I nearly stepped on you" She cried out.

"You, you little Buddha are in my bad books, what have you done with my little Doofy?" She asked the kitten in an agitated tone of voice.

Diablo just carried on rubbing himself against Miss Ruby Henderson's shins. "You won't get round me that easily," She added in a cross voice.

Miss Ruby Henderson sat down at her kitchen table, she leant on her elbows with her head in her hands, her bottom lip was starting to quiver, a single tear softly left the corner of her eye, it trickled slowly down the bridge of her nose until it reached the tip, where it formed a perfect droplet, dripping down in what could almost be described as slow motion, it hit the table, followed rapidly by cascades of tears.

"Wah..Wah..Wah"....Yes you've guessed it, she started wahring.

Diablo was sat on the floor, he quickly wiggled his bottom and sprang onto the table, he then started purring, he rubbed himself first one way and then the other against Miss Ruby Henderson's arms and face.

"How can I stay cross with you?" She asked the kitten cradling him in her arms. "You're mummy's little darling...Yes you are...Yes you are".

Diablo began licking Miss Ruby Henderson's wet nose.

"How could something as sweet as you have harmed my little Doofy?" She said lovingly to the kitten, who by now was wondering what could have happened to his dinner.

"Could she have forgotten?" Diablo thought to himself. "Meow..Meow..Where is my dinner?" He cried out.

"Ahh.. Do you want mummsie-wummsie to get you some foodee-woodee?

Do you want some foodee-woodee?" She said again placing the kitten on the floor and tickling his tummy.

Miss Ruby Henderson prepared the kitten's dinner.

"What's this then?...What's this then?" She said to the kitten as she presented him with a glorious bowl of food.

"Meow...Meow... I am not silly...I heard you the first time" The kitten said, plunging his face into the bowl.

"Phwoor!...Could that smell any worse?" Miss Ruby Henderson asked the uninterested kitten as she pinched her nose.

"Don't forget to wash hands after handling food stuffs!" She remembered. Just like her mother had told her.

"Buurp!..Exsqueeze me!" Cyril said as he belched, "I didn't think it possible... But I'm starting to feel more than just a little bit full-up," he told Amelie as he rubbed his bulbous belly.

"Wonders will never cease" she replied, "I never sought zat I would see ze day, Cyril ze great escapologist is finally full," she added.

"To bursting point," Cyril said rubbing his rather large girth again, "I don't feel so good...I think I may have a little sleep," he informed Amelie as he scratched his head. "Cyril!" Amelie screeched.."Your 'ead.. What iz 'appening to your 'ead?" The terrified female Caterpillar looked on in fear, her whole body started to shake and shiver.

"I really do need to lay down..Just for a while," Cyril moaned.

The frightened little Caterpillar started struggling to breathe, his whole body was starting to feel constricted by its own skin.

"Cyril are you okay? Per 'aps you should lay down," Amelie suggested as she grabbed his hands.

Cyril's whole body felt like a tube of toothpaste being squeezed from the bottom... With the lid still on!

"Owww my head!" Cyril groaned, writhing in pain.

Cyril's skin began to split down the centre of his head, Amelie saw this and screamed. "Cyril your e-e-'ed...urgh!" She fainted.

Cyril's skin started splitting even more, like an earthquake travelling across the countryside it tore down his back.

"Brrrrrrr," Cyril said in a shaky voice.."That was weird".

The slightly larger caterpillar shivered from the tip of his horns to the end of his tale, then like a child stepping out of a wet pair of trousers, he stumbled out of his newly shed skin. "I could eat a horse" he mumbled to himself, "Amelie check this out," he shouted to his friend.

He turned to see Amelie's body laying passed-out on a bed of Willow Leaves,

"Just getting your head down sweetie..good idea," Cyril said, patting the unconscious Amelie on the head.

Just then he spotted his reflection in the glass, Cyril scanned his new body up and down. "Looking good Cyril,.. feeling good Cyril," he said to himself as he admired his new skin. "Ooh are you talking to?" Amelie asked in a croaky voice.

"Um...No one," an embarrassed Cyril replied, "you fell asleep, You should have seen what just happened!" He added with an excited tone in his voice.

"I did" Said Amelie "It was 'orrible!... zat is why I passed-out".

"Check-out my shiny new skin... It's wicked!" Cyril boasted, "I feel like I could eat an elephant," the born again hungry Cyril said as he began munching on a mouthful of food. "You should not speak with your mouthful mon amore" Amelie insisted as she carefully removed a stray piece of Willow Leaf from her face.
"Sorry Shnookylumps," Cyril said.
"Shnookylumps!?...Ooh is Shnookylumps?" Amelie enquired in an angry voice.
"I have no idea," Cyril said "I must have got you muddled up with someone else".
"No doubt!...Anozzer girlfriend per 'aps!?" Amelie exclaimed.
"There has only ever been you my darling..My angel..My shnooky...Umm..Sweet, sweet Amelie," A more than a little bit confused Cyril said, "Could you pass me that Willow Leaf my darling? He asked Amelie.
"You must be getting me mixed up with someone else!" Amelie replied as she crawled angrily away.
"Fine then!".. Said Cyril "I will get it myself". "Go on zen!".. Amelie called back.
"Fine then... I will then!"... Cyril answered.
"Fine zen... Go on zen!" Amelie replied.
"Fine then!...This is me getting it myself.. I don't Know how I ever managed without you?" Cyril called back Sarcastically.
"'E will be back," Amelie thought to herself as she crawled off wiggling her Toosh suggestively.
"Don't think I don't Know what you are doing!..Or why you are doing it!" Cyril called out, "You are wasting your time!..No effect!..All I think about is my belly... remember?".... "Females..huh!..Who needs them?" Cyril thought to himself as he kicked the leaves with his rear feet of plenty.
He crawled around for a while feeling sorry for himself, then he accidentally bumped a twig that was leaning against the glass causing a cascade of leaves, covering him from horn to tail in large amounts of foliage.

"Help!..Help!"..He cried out at the top of his voice.

Amelie turned around immediately to see what all the fuss was about, but all she could see was Cyril's bottom pointing skywards...surrounded by leaves.

Amelie clambered cautiously over the mound of leaves until finally she managed to reach Cyril's bottom, when she saw it sticking out of the ground like a Stone-age Monolith it made her chuckle.

"It's not funny," Cyril said mumbling his words.

"Why are you mumbling?" Amelie asked in a curious tone of voice. "'Ave you fractured your jaw? Are zere any bones broken?"

"No..I've got...A mouthful...Of food!" He replied, chewing on still more leaves.

"Unbelievable..I sought zat you were seriously injured," Amelie cursed as she tutted to herself.

"So did I,"...Cyril moaned, "My sixth leg back took a bit of a knock from that twig, I think it's okay I can still move it, it's lucky you came when you did I could've been stuck for ages, it would've taken a long time for me to eat my way out of this lot......probably".

phaaarp!

"Cyril don't forget to keep away from ze wall, you just made it make zat spine tingling noise again," Amelie reminded Cyril in a shivery voice.

"Sorry!" replied Cyril, apologising for inadvertently cutting one "actually that was me that time... It was an accident!" Cyril's face turned a crimson red with embarrassment.

"What am I going to do wizz you?" Amelie asked holding her nose.

THuuuD!

Suddenly there was a loud noise as something impacted against the glass wall, both Caterpillars instinctively ducked down after hearing the loud thud. "What on earth was zat?" Amelie asked Cyril.

"That nearly frightened the life out of me!" Cyril answered. "Ow my nose!" A strange, squeaky voice said.

Cyril immediately grabbed hold of Amelie and pulled her in front of him.

"What on earth are you doing pulling me in front of you?" A shocked Amelie asked.

"I was not pulling in front..I was pushing to the side..Out of the line of fire..Duh!" Cyril replied, trying to make an excuse for his hiding behind Amelie.

Both caterpillars crawled tentatively towards the edge of the glass tank. "What is it?... Can you see?" Cyril asked Amelie.

"It would appear to be a small winged insect, It might be an idea to not let it see its reflection for a while," Amelie suggested.

"Why not?"...Cyril asked looking down at the injured bug, "Oh dear!...look at the state of that...Should its nose look like that?..And should it be there?" Cyril said, feeling just a little bit nauseous.

"Cyril try and show a little 'umility," Amelie snapped.

"Ow my head!" The little bug said as it clutched its nose.

That I should add was now squashed firmly onto the side of its face.

"It's okay...You are going to be okay....Try not to move," Cyril said slowly and precisely as he tried to comfort the injured insect.

"What is your name?" He asked the tiny bug.

"Havier...My name is Havier....My head hurts," groaned the little fruit fly. "Hello Havier...My name is Cyril and this is Amelie it's nice to meet you".

"It's nice to meet you too," Havier replied, "have you lived here long?" The fruit fly added. "Amelie and I have just moved in...Well I say just moved in...I used to live here before but I escaped...It was epic!...There's a book about it you Know... You should read it if you get a chance, it's mainly".....

THWAAAACK!

Before Cyril had a chance to finish his sentence..
Diablo the Kitten brought his paw down like a hammer onto Havier's head.
In one motion the pure evil Kitten swatted the fruit fly to the floor...Killing him instantly. "No!" Amelie screamed.

"Wooa!..Wooa!..Hold on a minute!...Four lines and that's it?..I'm dead!..
I was promised a speaking part...Not a parting shot...How many lines has the cat got?..And how much is he getting paid?..I'm going to have serious words with my agent!" The fruit fly says to the author,
angered by the fact that only a small part had been written for him.
"That's fine can we deal with this later, the plot is starting to thicken and I don't want to loose the reader's attention.. Thank you Havier for your co-operation".
The author writes adamantly in reply to Havier's questions.

"You have not heard the last of 'Havier the fruit fly'," Havier informs the author.

"I think we have...Amelie from the top"... The author writes insistently...

"No!" Amelie screamed.
"Diablo!..Its a Diablo!...Did you see that?!" Cyril screeched to Amelie. "Of course I did..I am not blind!" She replied abruptly.

"Don't move a muscle, I think they hunt by motion..If we stay purrfectly still it may not see us," Cyril explained to Amelie as he put his arm across her chest. "Meow...You are mine Cereal!...I will stalk you!.....I will pounce on you!..... And I will kill you until you are dead," the kitten said menacingly.

The Diablo fixed his gaze directly onto Cyril's face. "Do you think it saw us?" Cyril asked Amelie.

"I would not like to say zat it did not," Amelie replied, "Why isn't it doing any sing?.. It just sits zere googly-eyed...'e is looking at you Cyril, did you do some sing to tick 'im off!?" Amelie asked.

"I don't think so....Wait a minute!"....Cyril stopped and thought for a moment, he clambered onto a higher twig until his eyes met with the Diablo's, then he slowly turned his back and wiggled his bottom in the Diablo's general direction. "You can't get me... na na na na na!" Cyril chanted as he attempted to wind-up the kitten. "Are you crazy?..Ze Diablo will kill you!" Amelie shouted to Cyril at the top of her voice. "Don't worry it can't get through the wall that you cannot see...I remember...I used to do it all the time before," Cyril said.

"Before what?" Amelie asked.

"Before my epic escape...Have I not mentioned it before?...There is a book you know," Cyril answered.

Cyril stopped and thought for a moment, unsure as to whether he had mentioned it to Amelie before.

Tap..Tap..Tap...Diablo tapped on the glass with his razor sharp claw.

Cyril heard the tapping noise, as he scratched his head unsure of the source of the noise he turned to see the kitten pointing directly at him.

"Who me?..You want me?" Cyril said shrugging his shoulders and patting his chest. Diablo pointed at Cyril with one claw, while he gestured a crushing motion with the other. Cyril was however not really scared by this, he stuck his tongue out and started wiggling all of his limbs.

"Oh I'm sooo frightened....look at me....I'm wobbling in my Y-fronts," the daring little caterpillar said as he taunted the already angry Kitten.

"Meeoow...Hisss," Diablo cursed the little green caterpillar.

Swiping and slashing at the glass with his claws, the Diablo hissed again.

Cyril's juvenile actions where starting to have an adverse effect on Diablo's psyche, the Kitten was becoming more and more unsettled.

Diablo started to pace backwards and forwards in front of the tank, trying to formulate a new plan of attack.

Cyril decided it was time for him to take a little nap, but try as he might the tubby little caterpillar just couldn't get comfortable, the twig that he was perched on was more than just a little bit on the wobbly side.

"The twig on top of which I am perched, would appear to be, very much, a little on the wobbly side," Cyril said with a facetious tone in his voice.

This was so obviously a deliberate attempt to goad the author into an argument. However, unaffected by Cyril's pathetic, prodding with prose the author continued to write.

Cyril tried with all his might to lower his fat, little body, ever so carefully he tried to get down to the leaves below, only to end up hanging by his short, fat, boney, girly arms. "Umm Amelie.. I appear to be a little bit stuck," the obese caterpillar, with body odour, called to his pretty, female friend.

"Okay, I'm sorry," Cyril says apologising to the author, realizing his career could be hanging in the balance.

Swinging to and fro Cyril probed aimlessly with his tail searching for solid ground.

"Come on Cyril you can do this...Focus, be the ground," he thought to himself.

Cyril shut his eyes, took a deep breath and dropped.

Unfortunately Cyril became the ground a little quicker than he had anticipated, he fell like a sack of potatoes onto the floor of the tank.

"Ow that smarts!" He said grabbing three of his Knees, he began to slowly rock back and forth holding onto his three injured Knees, Cyril fought hard to stem the impending flow of tears.

"It doesn't hurt...It doesn't hurt," he muttered to himself.

Cyril started rocking himself faster in a vain attempt to stop the pain. Gripping his three injured Knees tighter, rocking back and forth faster, chanting quicker. "It doesn't hurt...It doesn't hurt," he started mumbling louder.

"Oh who am I Kidding, it really blooming hurts!" Cyril cried out doubled-up in pain.

"It would appear Cyril has actually suffered quite a serious injury, we should respectfully give him a couple of minutes to gather himself....And his belongings, if he is not to busy to stop blubbering like a baby that's lost its dummy, and do what he is paid to do!" The author writes callously.

"What do you mean blubbering like a baby? You would to if you had sustained injuries as serious as mine," Cyril calls out to the author.

*"let me see..Oh dear..Apologies... You have suffered what I can only describe as.. Quite light chaffing to areas confined about the Knees..And I mean that quite sincerely!..Now if you don't mind, can we get back to 'The big number two'?".*The author continues to write, unmoved by Cyril's constant crying of crocodile tears.

"No problem," an agitated Cyril replies.

The little...No Sorry... Now quite large Caterpillar stood cautiously onto his feet of plenty, "Ow!.. Ouch!..They are so sore you Know," Cyril said, briskly rubbing his three injured Knees.

"But I won't dwell on it...I will soldier on," The slightly larger Caterpillar said as he sucked on his bottom lip.

"Mon amore..Mon amore..What 'as 'appened to you?" Amelie asked Cyril.

"Oh It's nothing...Apparently it's just a little, light chaffing on three of my knees," he told her.

"Do you have any antistatic cream?" He asked Amelie.

"What is sis antistatic cream?..Does it 'elp stop ze build-up of friction on your knees while you are crawling?" Amelie enquired.

"No silly"...It stops the infection from spreading, that's why they call it antistatic....Duh!" Cyril replied in a patronizing voice as he rubbed Amelie's head.

"My poor brave Cyril," She said as she held Cyril in her arms of plenty.

"Do not worry mon amore.. I am 'ere now," she said, cuddling Cyril tighter.

Cyril started to try and walk unaided, on his own...And without the help of anybody else. "Woah!" He said as he tried carefully placing his feet of plenty one in front of the other. "Steady mon amie, you should not try to do too much...Too soon," Amelie said as she propped Cyril up against the nearest twig.

"You should rest a while and try to keep your weight off of zem," Amelie advised her poorly friend.

Cyril was quick to agree. Cyril thought for a while....

"Hey!..What do you mean weight?....I'm not fat!" Cyril snapped. "Much!" Amelie replied sniggering.

Miss Ruby Henderson walked into the hallway where she spotted Diablo, who was sat watching her caterpillars.

"Get down! You know you should not be up there...What have I told you?" Miss Ruby Henderson said as she wiggled her index finger at the kitten. She hurried over to Diablo and picked the kitten up.

"You're a little monkey...Yes you are...Yes you are," Miss Ruby Henderson said nuzzling the kitten.

Just then she noticed her caterpillars sat together in one corner of the tank. Miss Ruby Henderson crouched down holding the kitten and peered through the glass. "Oh no!..You've chaffed your knees...How did you do that then?" Miss Ruby Henderson asked, noticing Cyril's injured limbs.

"Oh no! Poor little Cereal"..Diablo meowed sarcastically, "diddums hurt ums knees?" The kitten added curling-up his bottom lip.

"My name is Cyril you always say it wrong," the slightly larger caterpillar commented.

"It's Cyril...C..Y..R..I..L.. Do you understand?" Cyril said spelling his name out to the kitten. "Or is it too much information for your little brain to compute?.. Does not compute..Does not compute," Cyril said as he moved his arms of plenty up and down like a robot.

"I know what I said Cereal!" The kitten hissed staring at Cyril with his pure evil eyes.

"You can stop that noise" Miss Ruby Henderson said putting the kitten down onto the floor and gently tapping his bottom.

"Meeoow...I'll be back Cereal!" Diablo hissed again.

"You should not antagonise ze Diablo Cyril," Amelie said fearing for Cyril's safety.

"But he was giving me the evils," Cyril answered, defending his actions.

Diablo jumped straight back onto the unit housing the glass tank.

"Meeooow..Meow..Meow, vengeance is mine Cereal!...Woo Ha Ha!" The kitten laughed, in the evillest of pure evil laughs...like a pure evil villain...Who was pure evil...

And who laughed a lot.....Pure evilly....

Miss Ruby Henderson slowly removed the tanks lid and gently lifted Cyril up to examine his injuries.

"They don't look that serious to me my little Romeo," Miss Ruby Henderson said in a comforting voice,"Let me put you back in with your little Juliet".

Miss Ruby Henderson carefully placed Cyril back into the tank next to Amelie. "Romeo and Juliet.....Seriously!" Cyril commented as he shook his head,"Of all the names she could have chosen," he added in total disbelief.
"Oh I do not know...I can sink of worse....Cereal" Amelie laughed. "Oh ha ha... You're not funny," Cyril remarked.

"Are you feeling hungry Amelie my love?" Cyril asked.
"Oui mon Ami are you going to prepare se dinner zen? She answered in a surprised voice. "Yeah sure I am, there you go!...Dig-in!" Cyril said as he pushed a pile of leaves towards Amelie, "It's your turn tomorrow!" He added quickly.
"Mercy beaucoup," Amelie said,"It is rare to see such devotion and dedication in an individual zeese days, ze way you apply your 'ole self to the task in 'and, wissout deviation is indeed commendable," Amelie said with a patronizing tone.
"That was what goes by the name of sarcasm these days...was it not?" Cyril replied. "'T'was," Amelie answered.
"I have said it before and I will say it again..You are not funny," Cyril commented.
Amelie started to laugh...Cyril started to eat...life was good...
They had there own home.
They had copious amounts of food.
They had more than enough space to swing a cat in, one careful lady owner. They had their health, and the one thing to cherish above all others.

"Have you guessed what it is yet?" The author asks.

"Yes!..That's it... well done...One Golden Minute"...The author is authorized to issue golden minutes... "Isn't he?" He asks.. Already knowing the answer.

"They had each other."
"Do you know I could never get sick of eating Oak leaves," Cyril informed Amelie as he took another big mouthful.

"I bet zat you could get sick...Especially with ze amount zat you eat!" She replied.
"No not me," Cyril said taking yet another large mouthful.

Phaaarp!

"Cyril you must remember to stay away from ze walls, zat noise is really starting to irritate me now," Amelie said in a shuddery voice.
"Sorry... that was me again...Sorry...It's all these greens I've been eating," Cyril Said, apologising for his misplaced trouser cough.

THUUD! PHaaaaaaarp!

The spine tingling noise echoed through the entire tank.
"Cyril do you mind I am eating!" Amelie said in a rather perturbed, angry voice.
"That one was not me...Well..Not that time," Cyril replied, trying to clear himself from blame.
Both Caterpillars turned around slowly...They heard a squeaky noise coming from the other side of the wall that you cannot see.
Cyril looked at Amelie... Amelie looked at Cyril...
They both looked at each other.
"I will handle this..I've had Special Forces Training," Cyril said pushing Amelie's face into a pile of leaves on the ground.
"Stay down and don't say a word," he whispered.
Cyril carefully applied a stripe of camouflage paint to each of his cheeks.
"Should zat not go on ze cheeks on your face?" Amelie asked in a confused voice.
"Oh yeah...Oops!...Silly me," Cyril said as he quickly put some of the paint on his face, "It's Just..It said..'Apply liberally to cheeks' on the tin...I thought it meant my but"
"I Know what you sought it meant!" Amelie said interrupting Cyril Just in the nick of time.
Cyril donned his red head band, tying it tightly at the back he turned to Amelie and gently Kissed her on the fore head.

"I've got this," the brave, slightly larger caterpillar said bravely, "should I not make it back...Just know I love you," he said with a tear in his eye and a lump in his throat.

Cyril lay down on the ground and slowly began to crawl forward, reaching cautiously with his arms of plenty...Ever forward he crawled, head-on into the grasping hands of danger.. Undeterred and unyielding he pressed on.

Cyril's little heart began beating faster, his little palms began to sweat.

But still...Undaunted...He moved forward into what could be the last action of his little life. "Try and keep your bottom down a bit!" Amelie called over to Cyril.

Cyril turned and whispered to Amelie,"Are you trying to get me killed?"..

"I told you to stay down and keep silent, we have no idea of enemy strength, or what kind of heat they're packing," he whispered in a quiet, trembling voice.

Cyril stopped and thought for a moment...

"Hold on a minute...I am rushing head-on into unknown danger, there could be hundreds... No thousands of enemies out there!" Cyril thought fearing for his life.

Cyril started panicking, but he could not let Amelie see how scared he was.

Cyril stopped and started to munch on some Oak and Willow leaves that were blocking his way.

Two minutes passed.. Three minutes passed... Four minutes had past....

Cyril was still making himself busy by enjoying an early evening snack. "What are you doing!?" Amelie whispered.

"I am replacing lost energy," Cyril whispered back.

"Cyril!..What about our impending doom!?" Amelie whispered through clenched teeth. "I'm dealing with it!..Can't I just finish the leaf I'm on?" Cyril whispered with his cheeks bulging with food.

Cyril started crawling once more.

His slightly chaffed knees were really starting to hinder his progress, he turned back to whisper to Amelie.

"I'm going to have to take a break…Just a small one," he whispered pointing at his knees, "My injured knees are really starting to give me Jipp"..He tried to explain,"crawling around on these leaves is just making them worse..I should be sitting down with my knees up…Taking it easy".

He proceeded to take another large bite from an Oak leaf. "Why are you whispering?" A squeaky voice asked.

Cyril jumped out of his skin.

"Well…Why are you whispering?" The voice asked again.

Cyril set about methodically eating the leaf that was blocking his view, eventually he managed to eat every leaf between himself and the edge of the tank.

Amelie started to grow tired of Cyril's inactivity.

"I am really growing tired of Cyril's inactivity," she thought to herself.

"I am growing really tired of your inactivity!" Amelie called over to Cyril. "Oh ha ha!" Cyril laughed, "that won't deflate my confidence…. much!" Amelie quickly crawled the four centimetres to where Cyril was laying. "Well what is it…Ooh is out zere?" She asked the slightly larger Caterpillar.

"I am eating…You told me not to talk with my mouthful," Cyril replied as he took another big bite from a leaf.

Amelie peered cautiously through the glass.

"It is just anozzer fruit fly, I cannot believe all ze fuss over a little, tiny fruit fly!" She exclaimed.

"Hi my name is Juan Pablo," the fruit fly called-out to Amelie.

Cyril reared-up onto his back legs and shouted-out in his gruffest voice, "Are you crazy?...I

could have killed you!" Cyril told the little fruit fly, Cyril quietly breathed a sigh of relief. "That was lucky it's just a little fruit fly," he thought to himself.

"You're lucky I didn't snap you like a twig!...I've had Special Forces Training you know..It's a Jungle in here," Cyril added puffing his chest out as he boasted to the little insect.

"So have I," the fruit fly informed Cyril. "So have you what?" Cyril replied. "Special Forces Training..I've had Special Forces Training too," the fruit fly told him, "I was attached to the 22nd S.A.S. Regiment at Hereford...Two tours in the Gulf.. What about you?" He asked Cyril.

"Oh..erm.. I don't play Golf... I mainly do about 200 'shups' and a bit of circuit training 'n' that," Cyril answered, trying hard to hide his embarrassment.

"Have you done any Black Ops?" Juan Pablo asked Cyril.

"Oh um.. Yeah..Black ones....Red ones.....Green ones..... And even some pink ones back in the day," Cyril told the fly.

"Uh?..I don't understand," the fruit fly said, baffled by Cyril's answer to his question. "I don't sink 'e does eizzer" Amelie added.

"I can't disclose the nature of any of the missions I have done...Um..They were classified... Um..Top Secret...Middle Secret..and umm..Bottom Secret," Cyril said in a cocky voice.

"You can tell me, I've got level 10-Red Security clearance," Juan-Pablo informed Cyril. "You would need to be way, way, way more levelled up than that.....And yellow at least," Cyril added trying not to blush.

"I sink zat you need to get your 'igh level, little yellow bottom out of ze 'ole you are in before you get into trouble," Amelie whispered quietly to Cyril.

Amelie crawled back into the relative safety of the leaves, closely followed by Cyril. "It's lucky Juan-Pablo identified himself when he did, it could have got very ugly, very quickly," Cyril said in a brave voice.

"Oh yes" Amelie agreed.

"You are a very lucky, 'ighly levelled, little yellow Caterpillar indeed".

Juan-Pablo tried heroically but to no avail to get to his feet, "Arggggh!" He shouted as he applied weight onto his injured limb.

His leg, sadly had been broken when he inadvertently flew into the side of the fish tank. He managed to get airborne just long enough to make it to the top of the tank, round and around he span struggling with his injuries.

"Bizz..Bizz.. Cyril.. Cyril!" He cried out in pain, "I need your help".

"How are we supposed to help you when you are right up there?" Cyril called-out to the fly.

"If 'e can make it to ze vent slots 'e could drop down into 'ere," Amelie told Cyril.

"If you can make it to the vent slots you could drop down!" Cyril shouted up to Juan-Pablo. "Roger that!" Juan-Pablo replied.

Juan-Pablo pulled himself across the glass ceiling of the tank to where the vents were, he then dropped down onto the nearest Oak twig.

However he was still feeling a bit groggy after his accident, he miss timed his jump and dropped like a stone to the floor.

Thankfully the dense foliage covering the tank's floor broke his fall. "That's gotta' hurt!" Cyril said holding onto his portly stomach.

Both Cyril and Amelie rushed to Juan-Pablo's aid.

Well...They moved as fast as there little legs could move their fat, little bodies.

Cyril was quick to lay Juan-Pablo into the recovery position, however the slightly larger

Caterpillar panicked about what he should do next.

Juan-Pablo grimaced as he pulled Cyril nearer to talk to him.

"It's no good buddy...I'm to banged-up...Took a big hit to my ribs...Think my splines all mashed-up...May have punctured lung"....

The badly injured bug struggled to breathe as he stuttered to instruct Cyril as to what he should do. "You're Gonna need to call it in buddy".

Slowly Juan-Pablo reached into his pocket.

"Watch-out!...He's going for a piece!" Cyril shouted diving on top of Amelie.

"It is a Two-way Radio!....Oh no 'e's got a Two-way Radio!" Amelie said sarcastically as she pushed Cyril off and rolled over onto her feet of plenty.

Juan-Pablo painfully passed the radio to Cyril.

"You'll need to call it in Cyril..I'm to injured," the fly said to the Caterpillar. "No problem," Cyril answered as he took hold of Juan-pablo's radio.

Cyril was dead excited, he'd never used a radio before.

"Charlie, alpha, sierra..mama's 'n' papa's..and foxtrot oscar," Cyril mumbled, all excited 'n' that.

"Radio Big Mamma...Immediate pick-up...Code name Solaris...Tangos are Oscar Mike"...Juan-Pablo said struggling to give Cyril the information.

"Pssst.. Amelie it's me...Havier," the Fruit Fly turned and whispered as he removed a fake moustache.

"'Avier I don't understand, what iss going on?" A slightly bemused Amelie whispered back. "I have spoken to my people...They then spoke to the author's people...

The author's people then spoke to the author..

His people then spoke to my people and they negotiated a better role for me.... He might write a second book you know...

Don't tell Cyril though..His head and his belly are big enough already," Havier told Amelie. He stuck the false moustache back on and winked, "mums the word".

Sensing the severity of the situation, Cyril put his mouth against the microphone of the radio.

"Hello this is Cyril..I've got a message for Juan-Pablo's mum.. Can she go to the shops immediately and pick up a Solero...Oh and two cans of Tango for his friends Oscar and Michael? Okay thank you".

"This is Big Mamma..Come in Solaris...Repeat last..Over"..The radio squawked. "Repeat last over what?..It makes no sense does it?" Cyril turned and asked Amelie. "Don't ask me I'm no espionage expert," Amelie answered.

Havier..."No, sorry"... Juan Pablo held his head in his hands, shaking it from side to side he muttered, "How on earth can Cyril mess that up..So unprofessional?" He thought to himself as he shook his head in disbelief... Again.

"What the.. How on earth did a fruit fly get in there?" Miss Ruby Henderson said sliding the glass tank's lid to the side, Miss Ruby Henderson reached into the tank and grabbed the
fly, squashing him quickly between two Oak Leaves.
"Oh yuk! there's only one place for you," she said holding her nose.
Miss Ruby Henderson rushed through to her kitchen, she quickly opened her back door and raced across her little patio to her pond.
"There you go Stripey..enjoy" she called as she placed the contents of the leaves onto a spider's web.

"You have got to be Kidding!" Havier..."*Sorry*"... Juan-Pablo shouted, "This was not in my contract!" He added in an angry voice in total disbelief of the position he found himself in.

"Oh sweets!" 'Fatima the Spider' called out gleefully at the top of her voice, sensing the fly was struggling to escape, she immediately darted across her web and with pin-point accuracy she activated her spinnerets, encasing the fruit fly in silk totally restricting his movements.
"Help me..Someone help me!" Juan-Pablo shouted as he struggled frantically.
"What a way to go!" The little Fruit Fly thought to himself,
"I've trodden the boards with Lord Larry O and Sir Johnny G...I'm so much better than this, I ought to be in pictures!" He called out, hoping someone...Anyone, would hear...Or care!

"*I mean it's Just a fruit fly who cares...Am I right, or am I wrong?*"..The author comments.

"I might be 'Just a fruit fly'..I do still have feelings, I've got rights you Know," Juan-Pablo protests to the author.

"Resista-manance is futile," Fatima informed the fly, sinking her fangs into Juan-Pablo's abdomen, with surgical precision she began to envenom-ate the poor, defenceless, little fruit fly.
"Ow that smarts!..That better not leave a mark," Juan-Pablo shouted, uncomfortable in what he thought was bad treatment by his agent.
"Help me!..Someone help me!...Hel...Ah," The fruit fly slipped into unconsciousness.

"Where do you sink the giant female walker 'as taken Juan-pablo?" Amelie asked Cyril. "Have you tried the Yew leaves with Melon?.. It's sweeet," Cyril answered with his cheeks bulging with food.

Diablo watched avidly as Miss Ruby Henderson left the Caterpillars unattended, straight away he sprang into action leaping up onto the dresser, he then stepped carefully onto the still unmarked pile of essays, using these as a launch pad he leaped across to the coat rack that was next to the unit that held the glass tank, the one containing Cyril and Amelie...His prey.
His powerful jump caused the pile of books to fall crashing to the floor.
Miss Ruby Henderson heard the loud thud that emanated from the house, she turned and started to walk back across the patio to her kitchen door.
"What on earth was that?" She thought to herself as she quickened her pace.

"Woah that was close!" Diablo thought to himself as he regained his balance atop the coat rack, Diablo quietly observed his quarry Cyril and Amelie, who were still feeding in the middle of the tank.
Cyril and Amelie still remained blissfully unaware of the kittens close proximity.
"Woo ha ha!...You are mine Cereal!" The kitten laughed menacingly to himself.
Diablo primed his leg muscles for the final pounce onto the glass tank, with a quick flick of his tail he leaped across the void landing on top of the tank with just a little hint of a skid, grabbing onto the now further open tank lid, he came to a body juddering halt.
Both Cyril and Amelie were frightened out of their little, green skins. "zat frightened me out of my little green skin!" Amelie exclaimed.

"I too am frightened out of my little green skin!" Cyril added.

"Don't you mean not so little green skin!" Amelie retorted as she tapped Cyril's rather large girth with her little arms.

"ze Diablo is back and 'e does not look 'appy!" Amelie said in a trembling voice. Cyril tried to hide Amelie under a pile of leaves.

"Stay there and don't move...I mean it this time!" The scared, slightly larger Caterpillar shouted.

"Cyril what are you going to do? You don't stand a chance against ze Diablo!" Amelie tried hard to warn Cyril about the futility of his endeavours.

"I will try to distract it, you must stay here and stay hidden!" Cyril said in his sternest of stern voices.

The brave, slightly larger Caterpillar took one breath before moving to join the frey.

Diablo had only one thing on his mind, to try and gain access to the Caterpillar's home, he pushed his furry arm and head inside the glass ceiling, running on the spot with his back legs Diablo attempted to propel himself further through the gap.

Still slashing up and down with his razor sharp claws, the pure evil pussy hissed frantically at Cyril.

"Surprise! Surprise Cereal...Guess who?.. Woo ha ha!" The Kitten meowed as he pushed harder against the wall of the tank.

"Nothing comes between a Caterpillar and his late dinner!" Cyril shouted, girding his loins for a head on charge at the little Kitten.

"You are mine Cereal.. Woo ha ha!" Diablo laughed menacingly again.

Cyril began to climb higher towards the Kitten Inch by inch the bold, slightly larger Caterpillar moved upwards..To destiny.

Without flinching, or for one second thinking of backing down, the brave and just a little foolhardy, slightly larger Caterpillar strode on undaunted by the danger unfolding in front of him.

"What not even a little bit?" Cyril says, questioning the direction in which the story line is headed.

"No!.. not even a little bit"...The author replies.

"Okay then," Cyril answers with a dry throat, fearing the worst.
Cyril soon reached the top of the twig, gripping onto the end with his back sucky feet of plenty, he reached for an adjacent twig that would take him higher, ever nearer his foe. "I think I may have to take a break for a bit," Cyril says.
"My knees....Don't forget my knees," he adds.

Unhindered by his previously injured knees, Cyril pressed on with the story line as instructed by the author.
"Seriously!.. I may pass-out if I don't stop soon," Cyril tries to explain to the author.

Un-phased by the light headed feelings Cyril still crawled on, like the brave, slightly larger Caterpillar we know he is.
"I really.. really do need to stop..I think my blood sugar levels are starting to drop," Cyril started bleat.

Unyielding, Cyril the slightly larger Caterpillar remained steadfast in both body and mind. "Seriously..I really feel I should have a bit of a lie down....Just for a moment.. or Just until I get my breath back....Please!" Cyril pleaded with the Author.

But Cyril sucked it all up..And like a true son of Sparta he would march on...
Forward into battle..No quarter would be given...
"Seriously.. You're still going to persist with this story line," Cyril says, feeling more than a little dejected,
"Okay, in for a penny in for a pound," Our leading character says. "lets do this!" Cyril sighed after taking a few energizing deep breaths.
"In through the nose..Out through the mouth," Cyril began chanting to himself.

It soon became only to clear to Cyril that the author would remain resolute in the writing of... What could be the last chapter of...'Cyril the short sighted Caterpillars'... Colourful life.

"I've Just managed to mention the title of the book..In the book, Kudos to me!" The author brags.

"Okay... This is it... For Liberty!.. For freedom!..And for the Brotherhood!..Cyril yelled as he began to run at full tilt towards the end of the Oak twig, diving with his arms out stretched he grabbed a thin piece of willow that was dangling in front of him, swinging around in a huge ark he headed directly towards Diablo's nose.

"BONSAI!" Cyril shouted at the top of his voice.

"Sorry Cyril don't you mean Banzai.... Bonsai is a dwarf tree"....The author writes correcting Cyril's mistake.

"I'm kinda in the middle of something right now!" Cyril says. "BANZAI!" Cyril shouted correctly.

The slightly larger Caterpillar tracked like a guided missile locked onto it's target, he held on for dear life as he swung nearer and nearer to....

"Diablo's open mouth!...I am swinging at full pelt...Holding onto a thin piece of willow towards the Diablo's open mouth!".... Cyril shouted in a panic stricken voice. Being eagle eyed, Cyril noticed right away how sharp and white the kittens teeth were, and WOW!.. how smelly his breath was.

"Don't Diablos use mouth wash?" He thought to himself wafting his hand across his nose. This action caused Cyril to loosen his already fragile grip on the Willow twig.

"No!" Cyril shouted as he started swinging totally out of control.

"Mummy... I want my mummy!" He screamed swinging closer to Diablo's widening smile. Cyril's short, chubby little arms and legs started flailing like he was climbing an invisible ladder.

"Unbelievable," Diablo smirked, all he had to do was open his mouth and just let the Caterpillar fall in.

"Oh yes!"... Diablo meowed menacingly, "Oh no!"...Cyril shouted all scaredy.

"What on earth are you doing?" Miss Ruby Henderson shouted grabbing Diablo by the scruff of his neck.

Cyril fell softly onto the leafy matt lining the tanks floor.

"That was done just in the nick of time thank you," Cyril says thanking the author.

"No problem, you didn't think I would kill you off just like that, did you?" The author replies.

"No of course I didn't...I mean, you wouldn't kill the cash cow would you?" Cyril says. "Of course I wouldn't.......Would I?" The author answers in an insidious tone.

"You are in trouble," Miss Ruby Henderson told the Kitten, "Is that what you did to my little Doofy?" She asked the Kitten in an angry voice. "Meeoow..Meow..Meow..I will get you Cereal..next time!" Diablo hissed.

"You can stop that hissing too," Miss Ruby Henderson told the Kitten.
Miss Ruby Henderson placed Diablo onto the Kitchen floor and shut the door. Diablo started scratching frantically at the closed door with his razor sharp claws. Like a dog digging for a buried bone, he would not stop until it had the desired result. "You will not stop me..Vengeance is mine!" Diablo meowed incessantly at the door.

Miss Ruby Henderson grew tired of the Kitten's constant scratching. Diablo remained resolute.
"I am Diablo...'Lord of the Kitties Realm'..I demand access right now..Do you hear me... I am like a lion..Hear me Roar!"
"WOO HA HA!" He laughed.

The skies started to darken, storm clouds began forming above the Kitten's head, crashing against each other they caused deafening rumbles of thunder.
Diablo the pure evil Kitten stood on his back paws with his front paws raised. "I AM DIABLO!...HEAR ME ROAR!...WOO HA HA!"
Making a spinning motion with his paws above his head, the Kitten conjured-up a fire ball. Then thrusting his right paw downwards, he launched it towards the door. Almost Immediately two massive lightening rods shot from the clouds, exploding at the base of the door with devastating effect.
"WOO HA HA!"...Again and again the pure evil Kitten laughed.

Diablo began randomly launching fire balls all around the Kitchen. He blew off the door to the Microwave,
He exploded the dishes on the drainer,

He bombarded his litter tray, with totally the wrong kind of bombs,
He blasted Miss Ruby Henderson's favourite pink love heart cushion into oblivion,
He turned to destroy Miss Ruby Hendersons picnic basket.
Miss Ruby Henderson's temper began to fray, she opened the kitchen door to confront the kitten.
"What is this all about? You will scratch all the paint off!" Miss Ruby Henderson said whilst rubbing her hand on the doors painted surface.
A petrified Diablo cowered away from Miss Ruby Henderson.
The pure evil little kitten was stuck to the spot, like a rabbit caught in a cars headlights. "Please don't tell me off" the kitten meowed.
Diablo began to rub himself against Miss Ruby Henderson, purring, as he weaved a mesmerizing pattern between her legs.
"How can I ever be cross with you?" She asked the kitten as she picked him up and tickled his belly with her nose.
"You are like putty in my hands..I can bend you to my will," the pure evil kitten purred.

"It's almost to easy..Just like taking candy from a baby," the kitten started purring faster, "This is the life," the young kitten thought, purring with glee.
Diablo stretched out his arms and legs, as though he were reclining on a hammock.
Miss Ruby Henderson held the kitten and walked through to the hallway.
Seeing the glass lid of tank halfway open, she closed it gently to keep the caterpillars safe. Durdle..der der..durdle..der der...durdle..der der der.
Miss Ruby Henderson's mobile phone started to ring.
"My phone is ringing..I will have to answer it," she explained to the little pussy as she put him down on the carpet.
Miss Ruby Henderson reached into the back pocket of her jeans and pulled out her phone. "It's Scott..I don't believe it," Miss Ruby Henderson said.
She turned quickly to check her hair-do in the mirror, feeling confident that it looked okay, she answered the call.

"Yeahlow," she said trying to sound all hip'n'that. "Speaking," she said.
"Oh Hi Scott...How are you?"...
"Fine..Fine..I'm fine, and you?..Just great," she thought to her self, "I have just asked him how he's feeling twice in one sentence". Quickly she changed the subject.
"How's your mum?" She asked.
"I don't believe it, why on earth would I want to know how his mum is?" Miss Ruby Henderson felt her cheeks starting to get redder and redder.
"Tonight.. Um I can't tonight..Um I've got a bun in the oven.. I mean a cake..I have a cake in the oven...I am baking a cake...Yes that's it, I'm baking a cake, I have a cake that is baking in the oven, that I have made..
No no not the oven, I didn't make the oven, I made the cake that I put in the oven, and the oven is baking it..
The cake that is in the oven is the one I made.. It's in there right now being baked, as we speak, it is being baked".
Miss Ruby Henderson started to get very flustered and really embarrassed, the longer the conversation went on the more embarrassed she got.
"Next Friday..Um yes..Next Friday should be good, I will have to check my diary for a window...Um yeah that would be good...Okay, speak to you Friday...Bye Scott".
Miss Ruby Henderson ended the call and looked into the mirror on the wall, as she made a funny face she started to moan.
"I've got a cake that I've made and it's in the oven baking, I made it myself, because I'm such a good cook, Oh yeah and I've made a soup starter from scratch and I've been busy all day marinading dead cow..To put in a silly casserole..
Or stew...
Or something else you eat that contains dead cow...Who am I kidding...I can't cook.... I don't even eat meat!"
Miss Ruby Henderson stomped through to her kitchen, frustrated with herself for missing out on a chance of a date with Scott.

She opened the cupboard containing her comfort foods.

She reached in and grasped a large bag of crispynoodledoodles.

"I've still got you," she said sadly, cradling the packet of crisps like a baby.

"Oh! I know what will make me feel better," she said to herself with a joyous tone.

Miss Ruby Henderson skipped across her kitchen...

Miss Rudy Henderson opened her freezer and spotted a large tub of ice cream, "Thank you Ben and Jerry®...You've saved my life," she said as she gazed lovingly at the tub.

With her body basking in a new, warm glow of contentment Miss Ruby Henderson grabbed the large tub of 'Chunky Monkey®'...Her favourite flavour..She closed the freezer door. Slamming the door shut... With her butt...She quickly reached for her favourite pink love heart cushion.

Cuddling the cushion, the crisps and the ice cream, she made her way through to the lounge, closely followed by Diablo.

She kicked off her slippers,

She schlumped Into her favourite spot on her comfy sofa,

She placed the large packet of crispynoodledoodles conveniently within her grasp,

She grabbed the Television remote control and pressed the stand-by button,

She then snuggled up to her favourite pink love heart cushion.

As Miss Ruby Henderson began to open the tub of 'Chunky Monkey®', her whole lounge was filled by Angelic choirs singing from on high, a brilliant burst of pure white light was expelled from the tub...Revealing the bananary, chocolatey and walnutty, heavenly goodness that lay within.

Quickly joined on the sofa by Diablo, she put her feet up to begin her fun filled Saturday night in.

"I will always have you," She said affectionately as she stroked her little pussy.

"She's like putty in my hands," Diablo purred.

The little Kitten started affectionately nuzzling up to the 'Chunky-Monkey®' ice cream pot. "It's not for you, it's mine mine mine..yes it is...yes it is!".. Miss Ruby Henderson chuckled, giving her little pussy a noogie.

Diablo realised he would have to up his game, so he started purring louder and faster. "Oh... Okay you can have just a little then," Miss Ruby Henderson said as she put a spoonful of ice cream onto the lid and placed it on the floor.

Diablo jumped down from the sofa to devour the ice cream.

The Kitten paused by the lid, just waiting for Miss Ruby Henderson to add another spoonful.

He sat down on the carpet right next to the ice cream pot's lid. He waited..

And he waited... And he waited....

Not normally being a big fan of waiting, Diablo started to get a little irate, Still waiting he looked at Miss Ruby Henderson...

He looked at the ice cream pot's lid...

He looked at Miss Ruby Henderson again...

Diablo started to think that maybe more ice cream would not be forth coming.

"You are joking right..Surely that's not it...That would not feed a fly!" Diablo meowed, "You have ten seconds to apply more ice cream to the bowl Human!" He meowed again. "Go on then silly, eat it," Miss Ruby Henderson said as she rubbed Diablo's head.

"Seven seconds!" Diablo meowed again.

"It will melt if you don't eat it," Miss Ruby Henderson said to the Kitten in a silly voice. "Five seconds, and I'm not Kidding!"... Diablo meowed a deeper meow.

"You will not get any more if you don't eat it," Miss Ruby Henderson said pushing the lid nearer to the Kitten's body.

"You now have less than three seconds to comply!" Diablo meowed patting the lid with his paw.

"Mmmm this is dee-lish!....You should try it," Miss Ruby Henderson said to the Kitten as she put another spoonful in her mouth.

"Right that's it!...Don't say you weren't warned!" Diablo hissed, pushing the lid over with his paw.

"Diablo you little Buddha...I will have to clean that up now!" Miss Ruby Henderson said tapping the Kittens bottom with her foot.

"I am Diablo..Hear me roar!....Woo ha ha!" the Kitten meowed, closely followed by a menacing laugh.

Almost immediately Diablo span around and scratched the bottom of Miss Ruby Henderson's foot.

"Ouch!..That hurts!" Miss Ruby Henderson shouted.

Diablo, recognising the tone of her voice shot out of the sitting room, through the Kitchen and out of his cat flap.

WAAACK!

Diablo lay in a fluffy heap on the floor holding his head, what the Kitten had failed to realise...Well he did but it was to late...Was the fact that Miss Ruby Henderson had locked the cat flap.

"Owww! My noggin," The pure evil Kitten meowed whilst he rubbed his head.

"That little devil!" Miss Ruby Henderson exclaimed as she gently rubbed her injured pinky. "I can't remember whether I unlocked the cat flap or not?" she thought, staring blankly into space, "Oh not to worry, I shouldn't think he wants to go out now anyway," Miss Ruby Henderson thought to herself, after pondering her quandary for a while she decided to resume her fun filled Saturday night in.

She continued to watch Television,

She continued to eat the large tub of ice cream,

She continued to devour the huge packet of crispynoodledoodles. "This is the life!" Miss Ruby Henderson thought to herself....

A single tear formed in the corner of her eye.... "This is my life?"

Meanwhile back in the Tank;

Amelie ran as fast as her little legs could carry her towards Cyril's lifeless body. The first thing she saw was Cyril's body laying motionless on the leaves.
Amelie started to fear the worst...Was Cyril dead?...
Was she destined to spend the rest of her short life alone?... Would there ever be another Cyril book?...
Was 'Persil®' better than 'Ariel®' at removing grass stains? So many questions... Would she ever find all the answers?

Amelie finally managed to reach Cyril's chubby, little body that was laying dormant amongst the leaves.
"Cyril my love...Are you okay?" She asked as she stared at the limp, listless body.
"why did you 'ave to act so brave and so fool 'ardy..Just to impress me?" She asked hoping for a verbal reply..Conformation that Cyril was still alive.
Amelie sat down next to Cyril's body, she reached forward and pulled his head to her chest.
"Oh why Cyril..why?" She asked herself rocking his limp body back and forth.
A tear trickled down her face onto Cyril's closed eye, this made Cyril sit up with a start. Cyril let out a mighty yawn, arched his back and stretched out his arms, as he looked lovingly into Amelie's tear filled eyes he held her hand and said...
"What are you blubbing about?"
Amelie let go of Cyril's torso causing him to drop onto the leaves with a thwack.
"What did you do that for?..You're the one who woke me up!" Cyril asked in a confused, cross voice.

"You could have injured me then!"…"Haven't I been injured enough already today!" The tubby little caterpillar added.

Cyril was always a little bit grouchy if he got woken up from a nap.

"I sought zat you were"…."Oh I don't know what I was sinking," Amelie answered as she wiped her eyes and had a good blow on an Oak leaf.

"You are weird, can't a Caterpillar take a nap?…Did you see me?.. I was awesome." Cyril started to explain how his training 'just kicked in',

"I was not scared or anything…If anything the Diablo was lucky, if the twig I was on had not snapped when it did….Coor!….I was that close to opening up a family sized can," Cyril added, gesturing a little gap with his arms of plenty.

"A family sized can of what? I don't understand," Amelie asked Cyril, still feeling a little weary.

Cyril just laughed as he continued to eat… And eat…

And eat…

"You really are a funny little Caterpillar," Amelie said as she joined Cyril in the demolition of yet another pile of leaves.

"Have you given much sought to your Pupation Period?" Amelie asked Cyril who was still focusing on just one thing...His mighty belly.

"Your Proposal of Pupation Period, Please clarify," Cyril said as he gradually spat his entire mouthful of food all over Amelie.

"I intend to form a Chrysalis, so ze 'olo-metabolic process can take place," Amelie told Cyril.

"The Holowhatnow?" A perplexed Cyril remarked.

"I am going to form a cocoon so my caterpillar form can change into a butterfly," Amelie tried to explain the whole process to Cyril.

"So where have you been hiding your magic wand then?..You don't have any pockets," Cyril asked.. His curiosity was growing with every word.

"You don't need a magic wand, your body will do it naturellement...Why do you sink you eat all ze time?" Amelie told him.

"I eat all the time because I get hungry, easily," Cyril quaffed.

"Well I am going to go and start my pupation now, you are welcome to join me mon ami," Amelie suggested.

"I will be along shortly...Just going to finish the leaves I am on.. Okay," Cyril said speaking with his mouthful.

Amelie started to ascend the nearest twig in the centre of the tank, the one that would afford her the best protection from predators, she climbed up to where the twig levelled out naturally with the ground.

"Ziss looks like a good spot," she thought to herself as she studied the twig formations. Amelie initiated the production of silk from the glands located on the inside of her mouth, after forming an almost perfect silk pad, she arched her back to attach her cremaster, hanging precariously by her tail, she curved her head upwards so she could apply more silk to the appendage.

With this part of the process complete she was simply left hanging, just like a bat in a cave.

"Peace at last," Amelie thought to herself breathing a sigh of relief. "Are you going to stay up there all night," Cyril called up to Amelie.

"I am going to stay up 'ere for as long as it takes me to transform," Amelie called back.

"So you won't be wanting any more leaves then?" Cyril asked with his fingers crossed. "No...you can eat all you like, I 'ave eaten enough," Amelie replied.

Cyril continued doing what he did best, he prided himself on how many leaves he could comfortably put away, in just one sitting, without including puddings.. This amount was beyond even Cyril's comprehension.

After what seemed like an age, Cyril decided to take a well earned break.

Phaaarp!

"Cyril I 'ope zat was ze glass!" Amelie snorted.

"Sorry that was me again....Sorry," Cyril replied appologetically, "Did I wake you?" He added.

"zat smell would wake ze dead!" Amelie answered holding her nose.

"It was an accident..It just slipped out....It's like it had a mind of its own," Cyril said feeling a little bit embarrassed.

"zat didn't just slip out...It rode out on a mighty steed!" Amelie replied.

Cyril decided it would probably be for the best if he joined Amelie on the Willow twig.. She looked lonely up there on her own...

And Cyril was unsure whether he...Sorry she, would like it up there all alone in the dark, so unselfishly Cyril started to climb the twig.

As Cyril got further up the twig it started to bow under the strain of his weight, he slowly and cautiously clambered up the twig towards Amelie.

After what seemed like forever, Cyril finally reached Amelie.

Panting like a dog that had just been on a long run, Cyril stopped to talk to Amelie. "I'm not as fit as I used to be," the unfit, little caterpillar puffed.

"You're not as sin as you used to be eizzer," Amelie sniggered.

"Don't be so unkind...I'm sure it's just middle-aged spread," Cyril said in a voice that sounded a little upset.

"Okay then.. How do I do that hookyupthingymawhat like you did?" Cyril asked.

"It iss easy, you just need to sink about what you want to do and your body will just do it," Amelie said, making it all sound so easy.

Explaining that all Cyril had to do was focus on what he wanted his body to do, and his body would naturally just do it, only made Cyril feel even more confused. This coupled with Amelie's explanation about how simple it all was, is where Cyril would probably fall short of the required skills set.

Cyril moved tentatively along the twig, so as to get just that little bit closer to Amelie. "Okay this is easy, all I hah hoo hoo hith hin hah how hith," he said with a mouthful of silk. He started to lick a twig, in a vain attempt to rid his mouth of silk. This was however only partially successful.

"Wow wah hoo hoo hin," Cyril asked Amelie feeling proud of his creation. Cyril turned to Amelie to see her reaction.

"Okay, now stick your Cremaster to ze silk pad," Amelie explained to him. "Stith maa whaa hoo on hurr burr brr?" Cyril asked.

His tongue was still a little bit tacky.

"Ze 'ooky sing on ze top of your derrière," Amelie replied.

"My dairywhatnow?" Cyril asked with a confused tone in his voice.

"The hooky thing on the top of your bottom!" Amelie exclaimed, getting more impatient with every second that passed.

"On top of my bottom!..It makes no sense," Cyril said, now he really was baffled.

"Are you sure you know what you are doing?" He asked again.

Cyril scratched his head...

Cyril then scratched his bottom...

"What on earth is that hooky thing on my..Oh!.. I get it," Cyril said noticing his Cremaster appendage on the top of his tail.

"This is a piece of cake...I can handle this," Cyril said as he attempted to hook himself onto the spun silk pad.

"Waaaaah!"

Thuuuummp!

Cyril had unfortunately, totally missed the silk pad he was aiming to hook onto, instead he just fell head first into the pile of leaves on the floor below.

"Ow zat 'as got to 'urt!" Amelie winced.

"Ow that hurts!" Cyril said clutching his melon.

Cyril had landed smack, Bang on his noggin and his tail end was now wafting, listlessly left and right, Just like a Concertina.

In-fact...He looked exactly like a battered, old wizards hat that had been left on a bench.

Cyril stretched his legs out causing his body to flop over onto its side, he then remained prone on the leaves for a short while trying to regain his composure. Amelie hung upside down trying to fight back her tears, her whole body shook through trying not to laugh and cause Cyril any undue embarrassment.

"I cannot believe I have got to climb that twig again," Cyril called to Amelie, hoping she would give him a reason not to have to do it again.

Noticing Amelie had tears in her eyes, Cyril scrambled to his feet of plenty. "It's okay... I'm okay...look.. I'm fine," Cyril said doing a twirl.

Regaining his balance, after a little bit of a dizzy spell, Cyril once again started to climb the twig towards Amelie.

He was beginning to wonder whether the whole pupation period was worth all the walking, or all the climbing, his feet of plenty were really starting to ache.

"You need to 'urry up Cyril!.. I sink some sing is starting to 'appen!" Amelie cried out in a panic stricken voice.

"No problem...I am here," Cyril said as he carefully hooked his rear appendage onto the silk pad.

"GERONIMO!"

He shouted throwing himself bravely off of the twig.
Like a humans first attempt at a bungee jump, his fear was soon replaced by euphoria.
"Did you see that Amelie, it was wicked!" He yelled at the top of his voice.
"I could 'ardly miss it...You missed me by millimetres and I 'ave a ringing in my left ear now!" Amelie replied.

"Sorry I got a little excited, what happens now?" He asked.
"Um Amelie, I can feel all the blood rushing to my head," he added as his face turned a flushed, crimson red colour.
"Just relax and let ze good feelings wash over you, imagine you are under a waterfall or Just dancing bare foot srough ze long grass...It's so beautiful," Amelie whispered with glee. "Yeah, I'm sure it's all groovy baby and all psychedelic and that, but my head aches," Cyril said.
"How long do you think we have to hang here?..It's Just, I am starting to get hunger pangs...
How long ago was it I last ate Amelie?..... Well, how long do you think?..
Amelie...Amelie...Am I talking to myself?" The chunky little Caterpillar asked.
"Amelie...Amelie!" He repeated over and over.
Amelie had fallen into a deep slumber.
"Great..Just hanging with my peeps, upside down, stuck by my bottom to a twig..
Bored!...Bored!...Bored!"...Cyril said speaking to himself.
Cyril began gently swinging himself backwards and forwards.
"You Know I'm bored..I'm bored..I'm really, really bored," he started to sing.
Just then he stopped himself from swinging..From his elevated position Cyril could see the Melon slices.
"Melon, mmm," he moaned all forlorn.
Cyril's whole self became swathed in melancholic pathos.

"My whole self is swathed in melancholic pathos and stuff!"...And I am really sad and lonely, don't forget that"...
"Oh, and I'm a little bit hungry too," the chunky, slightly larger Caterpillar added.

"It's puppy fat..I will lose it when I'm older!"
Cyril says getting just a little lippy with the author.

"Don't worry I don't think anybody will forget that, All you have talked about over the last few pages is how sad and hungry you are".The author added, hoping Cyril would just do the job he's paid for.... *"And stop being so lippy!"* The author writes.

Cyril stopped and thought for a moment..
"Was there much work out there for a short sighted caterpillar? And what kind of work do caterpillars do anyway?"

Thankfully common sense would prevail and Cyril will continue to apply himself one hundred and ten percent to the job he gets paid for. The author writes seeing Cyril deep in thought.
Cyril rocked back and forth...Back....And forth...Back....And forth...Just like a pair of pants drying on a washing line, swaying on a Summer Breeze.
"Sweet days of summer the Jasmines in bloom..July is dressed-up and playing her tune,". Cyril sang...shredding some sweet chords on an air guitar.

"If Cyril could stop rocking-out for a moment..And pay attention to Amelie, He may notice she is starting to Pupate!" The author writes, in hope that Cyril would concentrate on the story.

Cyril stopped rocking-out for just a moment...Suddenly he realised Amelie's skin was starting to split down the centre of her forehead.

"Oh no!...I have Just stopped rocking-out for a moment...And I can't help but notice Amelie's skin has started splitting down the centre of her noggin," Cyril said with a facetious tone in his voice.

"Oh my life!... Amelie's skin is actually splitting down the middle of her head!" Cyril said thrashing about on the twig anxiously

"Amelie's skin is splitting!.. Amelie's skin is splitting!" A terrified Cyril shouted. Quickly realising he could do nothing to help Amelie's plight, Cyril started to sob uncontrollably.

Amelie's skin ripped like a news paper from her head to her tail, only to reveal Amelie's beautiful, perfectly formed Chrysalis.

"Her face!..What has happened to her face?!" Cyril started to scream, shocked by what had Just happened.

Cyril Just hung upside down on the twig quietly shedding a tear for his beloved Amelie. "Why!..Why did you have to write that bit into your stupid book?" Cyril asks the author as

he starts to whale like a Banshee.

"I wrote that bit in my stupid book because that is what happens to a Caterpillar when it enters it's Pupation stage of life, it sheds it's skin to reveal a Chrysalis, the Chrysalis then hardens in the fresh air. Inside the Chrysalis the Caterpillar's whole body breaks down to a cellular state, these Imaginal cells then re-assemble in a different order to form what emerges from the Chrysalis or 'eclose' as a butterfly. This complete transformation is Known as holo-metabolism, does that answer your question as to why it is in my 'Stupid book'".The author explains.. Trying to put Cyril's mind at ease.

"No no, I never signed-up for this!"

"I want you to write me and Amelie out of this whole pupation story line"... "Right now!"...

"I've seen enough thank you"...
"Time-out"...."We need to take a time-out"...
"Can't we Just sit down, put our heads together and see if we can come up with a different story line....
Please!" Cyril pleaded with the author.

"I am sorry Cyril but that's the story, 'This is your life' and I am afraid that's nature..It's out of my control...Chin-up you'll be Joining Amelie soon," The author writes trying to console Cyril.

Cyril started crying and pleading with the author. "Please..Can't you Just get us both down from here?"
The little caterpillar looked really sad, Just hanging there, swinging to and fro. Tears ran freely down his head onto his horns, from there down to the leaf litter lining the aquarium's base.
Cyril continued to swing.
Cyril carried on blubbing, so much so his nose ran into his eyes.
By now Cyril could barely see anything, his eyes were just a collage of tears and snot. Cyril started to sing.
"We can start over again".... "Grow ourselves new skin".... "Buy a house in Devon"....
"Drink cider from a lemon...lemon...lemon"...

"Hi Cyril sorry to be a pain, but I think you will find the lyric is 'Drink cider from eleven', Not 'lemon', like you sang". The author writes pointing out Cyril's mistake. "OKay Cyril... let's take it from the last line..OKay?". "Cyril, OKay?!"...
"Cyril!"... "Cyril!"...

'Fade to grey'

Lightning Source UK Ltd.
Milton Keynes UK
UKIC01n2218140715
255208UK00008B/45

* 9 7 8 1 4 9 9 0 9 6 7 4 3 *